HOME ON THE RANGE

Brian Ajhar

Dial Books for Young Readers 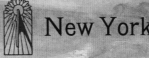 New York

Published by Dial Books for Young Readers
A division of Penguin Young Readers Group
345 Hudson Street
New York, New York 10014
Designed by Jasmin Rubero
Text set in OPTI Baltimore
Music set by Robert L. Sherwin
Manufactured in China on acid-free paper

1 3 5 7 9 10 8 6 4 2

Library of Congress Cataloging-in-Publication Data
Ajhar, Brian.
Home on the range / by Brian Ajhar.
p.   cm.
Summary: In this illustrated version of the familiar song, a young boy
is transported from his city apartment to life on the range.
ISBN 0-8037-2918-9
1. Children's songs—Texts. [1. West (U.S.)—Songs and music. 2. Songs.] I. Title.
PZ8.3.A296Ho 2004
782.42164'0268—dc21
2003010403

The art was prepared using acrylic paints and drawing pencils on
pressed paper and illustration board.

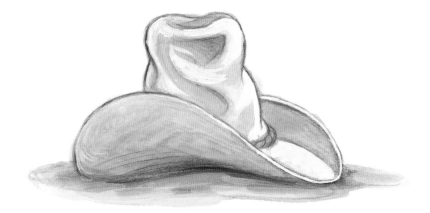

To our budding artist . . . Andrea

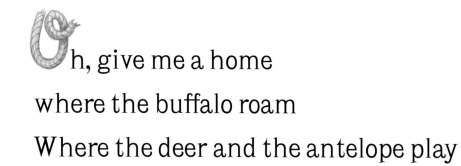Oh, give me a home

where the buffalo roam

Where the deer and the antelope play

Where seldom is heard

a discouraging word

And the skies are not cloudy all day

Home, home on the range

Where the deer and the antelope play

Where seldom is heard a discouraging word

And the skies are not cloudy all day

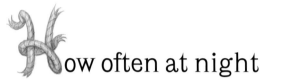ow often at night

when the heavens are bright

With the light from the glittering stars

Have I stood there amazed

and asked as I gazed

If their glory exceeds that of ours

Home, home on the range

Where the deer and the antelope play

Where seldom is heard a discouraging word

And the skies are not cloudy all day

Where the air is so pure,

the zephyrs so free

The breezes so balmy and light

That I would not exchange
my home on the range
For all of the cities so bright

Home, home on the range

Where the deer and the antelope play

Where seldom is heard a discouraging word

And the skies are not cloudy all day

Oh, I love those wild flow'rs

in this dear land of ours

The curlew, I love to hear scream

And I love the white rocks

and the antelope flocks

That graze on the mountaintops green

Home, home on the range

Where the deer and the antelope play

Where seldom is heard a discouraging word

And the skies are not cloudy all day

HOME ON THE RANGE

2. How often at night
   when the heavens are bright
   With the light from the glittering stars
   Have I stood there amazed
   and asked as I gazed
   If their glory exceeds that of ours

3. Where the air is so pure,
   the zephyrs so free
   The breezes so balmy and light
   That I would not exchange
   my home on the range
   For all of the cities so bright

4. Oh, I love those wild flow'rs
   in this dear land of ours
   The curlew, I love to hear scream
   And I love the white rocks
   and the antelope flocks
   That graze on the mountaintops green